C 17

BRAIN CAMP

First Second

New York & London

Text Copyright © 2010 by Susan Kim and Laurence Klavan
Illustrations Copyright © 2010 by Faith Erin Hicks

Published by First Second
First Second is an imprint of Roaring Brook Press,
a division of Holtzbrinck Publishing Holdings Limited Partnership,
175 Fifth Avenue, New York, NY 10010

All rights reserved

Distributed in Canada by H. B. Fenn and Company Ltd.
distributed in the United Kingdom by Macmillan Children's Books,
a division of Pan Macmillan.

Design by Colleen AF Venable

Colored by Hilary Sycamore and Sky Blue Ink

Cataloging-in-Publication Data is on file at the Library of Congress.

ISBN: 978-1-59643-366-3

First Second books are available for special promotions and premiums.
For details, contact: Director of Special Markets, Holtzbrinck Publishers.

First Edition August 2010
Printed in January 2010 in China by
South China Printing Co. Ltd., Dongguan City, Guangdong Province
1 3 5 7 9 10 8 6 4 2

BRAIN CAMP

WRITTEN BY SUSAN KIM & LAURENCE KLAVAN

ARTWORK BY FAITH ERIN HICKS

COLOR BY HILARY SYCAMORE

:01

First Second

NEW YORK & LONDON

Elevation, 18 degrees... angle, 38 degrees... going north by north-west, it should be right over...

Bingo.

...Two minutes, eighteen seconds.

No fair, Clerkson... I was here first.

Meanwhile, across America...

Faster!

Focus!

Higher!

Swing low to high!

In the suburbs of New Jersey...

Your daughter is brilliant.

I can't believe she's starting Yale this fall... at fourteen!

So, who's next?

We haven't heard from Jenna yet.

Yes! Dr. Chun... where's Jenna?

Where's Jenna?

Guess there's no point delaying the inevitable...

Bring out Jenna!

It's her turn!

No, fair prince... I shall drink the poison from the chalice in order that you might live!

Why is your sister so retarded?

In Queens, New York...

$2.99

Mrs. Meyer, I'm Mr. Oswald.

I'm from Camp Fielding, America's best new educational summer camp, guaranteed to prepare any child for the SATs and beyond.

Sorry for the late hour.

Well, yes, it is after ten...

We've had two campers withdraw unexpectedly. Based on profiles submitted by schools, we've chosen Lucas for one of these open slots.

I need some coffee.

...chosen Jenna for one of these slots.

But she got turned down for math camp, computer camp, art camp...

But Lucas has never done well on a test in his life.

We're looking for those with room to grow— late bloomers. Let me show you.

Given the program's fast pace, we need him there by tomorrow. Can you do that?

Well, it's a big decision, my wife and I need to discuss this...

I understand... thank you for your time.

You're going?

I'll be sure to thank Dr. and Mrs. Park for the referral.

Wait a second!

You're that place the Parks sent their daughter to last year?

They've been raving about it... and now Stella is going to Yale! At age fourteen!

You're that camp that was on Oprah? I tried finding you guys online, but—

It's by invitation only. Good night.

Wait!

Come back!

So what did you and that guy talk about all night, Ma?

Oh, just grown-up crap, that's all.

Try not to humiliate me, okay?

C'mon... we got a long drive ahead of us!

HONK

I still don't know what the big hurry is...

So what were you and that guy talking about all night?

Oh, just contract stuff...pretty boring. You didn't miss much, honey.

P FIELDING LEARNING AND FUN!

EARNIN

...and those are your bunks...

What's that?

Uh... that's our herb garden. We just fertilized.

Tennis, golf, and gymnastics every morning at nine; and swimming's at two on the T-days.

The what?

Nerd.

Gangsta wannabe.

The T-days. Tuesday, Thursday, and Saturday. Swimming's at two on the T-days.

They're both here... so we're only six days behind...

Good. Very good.

What the—

SLAM!

Umm, Effingham...

I'm sure you didn't realize it, but that's actually my pillow.

Get bent, limpo.

But you can't want a pillow with my cooties. Why don't you buy a nice new one? Would, say—

—twenty-five bucks be enough?

SMACK

What'd you pay him for? You shoulda kicked his fat ass.

It's a small price to live to fight another day.

I'm Dwayne. Welcome to a world without puberty.

I'm Lucas.

Are you replacing Clerkson? That was fast.

What happened... he couldn't hack the work?

Are you kidding? He was the smartest kid in Cabin 3. That's the cabin where the genius boys are—

—which is strange, because last week, I swear they were all exactly like him.

Meanwhile, at the girls' cabin...

GIRLS' CABIN

BOYS' CABIN

POOL

Yuck, gross, eeeyew, ick...

Hi... I'm Jenna.

I'm Sherry. Are you taking over for Tiffany?

...I guess. Who's Tiffany?

Like only the smartest girl in Cabin 6. Cabin 6 is the smart cabin. This is Cabin 4. We're all stu—

Hey—who's Raisin Boobs?

...oops!

SQUISH

Uhh...
ohh no...
ohmygod...
unnnhhhhh...
urrghhhh...

ARGHHHHHH

Sshh... don't worry, it's no biggie...

But what is it?

Ohh... it's just a baby bird. Musta fallen out of its nest. Just don't think about it, okay?

SQUISH

So. You ready for some lunch?

What is it, anyhow?

I dunno. Chicken? Oatmeal?

I'm a vegetarian. Excuse me? Do you have anything vegan?

GLORP

They have these huge boxes of powder in the kitchen. I think that's what everything's made of.

Does it taste as gross as it looks?

I wouldn't know...

I'm allergic to almost everything. Even a smell can trigger it. My whole head balloons up. My throat even seals off.

Stop, I'm starving.

But—what—you're all right?

Great. You know why? I'm alive!

I'm still starving. Man, I could go for a hamburger

I could go for the paper the hamburger comes wrapped in. Let me see what I can dig up...

Growl...

...Ohmigod!

Hey.

Where'd you get that?

Get what?

They're stale, but at least I killed most of the ants... Hey... a Balance bar!

I saw it first!

We can share it... c'mon!

Are you both high? It's mine!

SPLAT

Nice going, you... stupid morons!

Sorry. And that's redundant.

What?

What you said. Morons are stupid. So it's redundant.

I thought you were supposed to be dumb.

I am.

So am I. Actually, I'm secretly "bright" but for some reason I'm a real "underachiever."

Underachiever... nice to meet you. I'm a "lazy slacker" with a "bad attitude."

—and I'm "hyper" and "clueless."

Okay, people... listen up!

You get five minutes to finish up. Then it's time for the afternoon's activities!

Trust me... she doesn't mean volleyball.

The weird thing is, they don't teach at Camp Fielding. All they do is throw you into a subject and figure you'll just pick it up.

$(\sqrt{7})^2 = r^2 + r^2 - 2rr\cos\left(\frac{2\pi}{3}\right)$

Which is a really weird way to teach someone.

Kunt u wat ik begrijpen zeg?

See what I mean?

So who's that?

Cabin 3. And that's 6 right behind them.

No way... a giant maze? I hate mazes...

MAZE

Okay, Jenna... you're next!

But I'm no good at directions! I get lost in my own school! Please don't make me!

I can't find the way out...

C'mon.

Okay, you two. This way. Two hours and fifty-three minutes. Congratulations, Sherry... it's a new record.

Thank you.

Is it just me, or is dinner even grosser than lunch?

Yo... attention everybody!

Oh man... is that what I think it is?

Ice cream. But don't get your hopes up.

And the winners of today's games: the girls of Cabin 4!

VANILLA

We won? But we really sucked!

Yes, Sherry. You won. Now enjoy it.

I swear, they do it to torture us. They only pick one winner a night.

Thank you, that's very nice! Don't mind if I do!

Hey!

What happened to yours?

Hey Sherry? Sherry... wake up, there's something out there!

BAM BAM BAM

Do you have any aspirin? My head is killing me.

Me too. And I had the hardest time waking up, it was weird...

Oh my god.

Eeeyew... gross!

What is that? What's on my head?

How should I know? Get away from me, you're disgusting!

Look— you got one, too!

Eeeyew! Yuck, help me! Come on!

SQUISH

SQLOOSH

Hey, guys—don't worry about me, I just slept on the ground...

BATHROOM

Would you quit blocking the way, freak?

Where'd she go?

Who?

Sherry.

Home. She had a family emergency.

She did? When?

This morning. Her...her mother is sick. But don't worry, I'm sure she'll be fine. Breakfast in ten!

Lucky.

Oww!

Ohhhh no...

This must be it. I can't believe this...

Look... I bet she's going for more of her food stash.

Unbelievable. Here, of all places...

Doesn't anybody have anything...?

SUPPLIES

Thank God!

Wha—?

?

Hey... that's mine!

I thought you had more food!

Well, I don't!

Meanwhile...

Better. Already. Hey... who's missing?

The new girl. Jenna.

And she slept outside last night.

What's this a map to?

Is that what you do at home... just steal stuff?

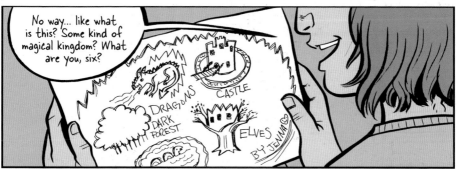

No way... like what is this? Some kind of magical kingdom? What are you, six?

DRAGONS

CASTLE

DRAGONS DARK FOREST

ELVES BY JENNA♡

For your information, I'm almost fourteen!

Serious? Me, too.

I wish this was a real map. Then I could run away from here. To someplace civilized.

Well... isn't there a Snack Shack right down the road?

So? Even if there is, I don't have any money. Do you?

No. But I know someone who does...

Well, it is my "Save My Life" fund. But if you get me some chocolate...

So where exactly is it?

On the big road by the exit.

Okay... that's Highway 7. It runs east-west.

You go this way through the woods... that should get you to a dirt road... turn right... and you're there.

Only you're coming with us.

No way. I'm not having you drag me through the woods... it's hard enough getting around on asphalt.

Well, we'll go slow then.

Yeah. No problem!

Look, it's not just that... you don't know my parents. This is like the millionth camp I've been to. If I screw up here, they said they're gonna ship me off to some boarding school in Switzerland...

Don't worry, we won't get caught... we promise.

CRACK

AGH!

A deer.

It's just a deer.

Whew.

Ticks! Ticks! Check yourself for ticks!

There are windows out back. Let's see if they're open.

Did you see anything? Like a soda machine?

I couldn't see much. Could you?

No.

It's like the nursery at a hospital. Let me see what else there is...

AGGHHHHHHHHHH!!!!

Ohmygod... there's kids in there!

Here, try to get on the ledge...

Aauugghhh!!!

Ohmygod...that was Sherry!

And Clerkson... and Tiffany! But they went home!

Look—they're over there!

Not that way... there are more coming!

Aghhhhh!!!

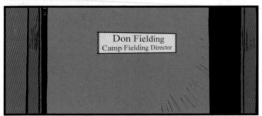
Don Fielding
Camp Fielding Director

So. Jenna, Lucas, and Dwayne.

What are you going to do with us?

What do you mean?

We want to go home!

Is that what you really want?

Well, yeah! We saw a — oww!

A what? Did you see something that upset you?

...No. Just a building.

We're only trying to help you. Lucas... do you really want to up in prison, like your dad? And Dwayne... I bet boarding school isn't much fun, is it? And Jenna...

...how does it feel when even your baby sister is embarrassed to be seen with you?

So I bet you don't want me calling your folks, right?

No.

No.

No, Sir.

He's letting us go, just like that?

And what was that about eating? He sounds like my grand- mother.

Okay, then... no harm, no foul. Let's just pretend none of this happened, okay? Besides... you'll all feel a lot better once you eat and get some sleep.

Ohmygod— look.

So?

TOMMY'S HOUSE OF PIZZA

My mom calls this a "ten-finger discount."

Why *didn't* he call our parents? You think he's scared we might tell them what we saw?

Like my Mom would ever take my side against any adult.

Yeah. Knowing my folks, I'd probably end up grounded.

But we don't even know what we saw. A bunch of kids yorking up feathers. Maybe it was nothing.

Yeah, right. It happens every day...

Hey... I just thought of something.

A zillion years ago, there was this girl and her mom staying at this hotel. One day, the girl decides to go out shopping...

What? What girl?

It's a story.

So the girl goes shopping and comes back, only her mom's gone. Like vanished.

So the girl complains, and the hotel people go, like, what are you talking about?

And she goes like what happened to my mom? And they go, you don't have a mom...

...you came here by yourself. And she goes oh yeah? And they go yeah. And then she goes—

Back up. What are you getting at?

Shut up, I'm almost finished.

And they go, okay, so what room did you stay in? And she goes, room 414. And they go, we don't even have a room 414. And she goes oh, yeah?

Only when she goes up to the fourth floor...

60

413

They're right. There's absolutely no room 414 anymore. Just a blank wall.

So what happened to the mom?

She died of the plague. Only the hotel didn't want anybody to know... so they sealed up the room and pretended it didn't happen.

So what are you saying? Those kids back there have the plague?

Okay, so like maybe not the plague. But something like it.

Yeah. Like "feather-itis!"

And Fielding and those guys can't risk anybody finding out about it. Or else this whole place would be ruined.

That's crazy...

So just because some thing's crazy it can't be true...

The first thing we should do is get those three kids out.

Just us? How?

Yeah... Fielding's going to be watching us like a hawk.

I can jimmy a window... that's easy. We can do it tomorrow, when nobody's looking. We just have to convince people to help us...

But who's going to believe us?

I don't know. But what choice do we have?

Okay. If you guys take your cabin, I'll do mine!

So how can you seal up a door and paint it while someone's out shopping?

Wouldn't it still be wet?

It's a story. Besides—just because something's crazy doesn't mean it can't be true.

But Clerkson went home.

Yeah. He had a family emergency...

But did you see Clerkson leave? Did you actually see him get into a car, say goodbye, anything?

We think maybe they're sick... like with the plague.

No way!

The plague!

Are you serious?

What's the plague?

So what do we do?

First off—we have to break in and get those kids out. They need a doctor and we need some answers.

When are we talking?

Tomorrow morning... during Mind Maze. We can break away in groups of twos and threes.

Hi, Jenna.

... Uhh, hi...

Hi, Jenna.

Hi, Jenna.

Hi, Jenna.

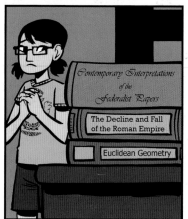

Contemporary Interpretations of the Federalist Papers

The Decline and Fall of the Roman Empire

Euclidean Geometry

Hey, umm—

—are you like... okay?

Yes, Jenna?

Certainly. Why do you ask?

Because—because I'm starting to think something maybe kinda weird is going on around here?

Weird?

TWITCH

Lucas, Dwayne, and I were in the woods, and we found something really bizarre. It's kinda like a, ummm...

Go on. What did you find?

... a laboratory. I think. And, umm, we also think we saw Sherry in there... and we think maybe she's sick, really sick I mean...

Sick? You think Sherry is sick?

67

It's my bunk. I think everyone's infected... look.

Care to join us?

So we'll just do it with the guys, that's all.

Don't worry. It's gonna be okay.

Dwayne's late. We better save him some pizza or he'll be mad.

We should head back, before anyone notices.

What the—

That night...

BOYS' CABIN
GIRLS' CABIN
POOL

Holy...

ZZZZzz   zZZ...

CRUNCH

CLIC

Shh... not so loud, Ty.

Are you kidding? They're dead to the world.

Watch it.

Got it.

Just the top bunk...

Watch out!

CLANK

Real sterile, Ty. You're a natural.

Shut up. At least it beats flipping burgers this summer, right?

Hey Dwayne?
You okay?

In the morning...

MAZE

All ready to go? Hey—are you okay? You look awful.

Something weird happened last night and I—

Focus, people!

Three minutes, two seconds.

Yes!

... four minutes and four seconds.

... Dwayne? Are you okay?

Of course I am. I feel great.

You do?

Yeah! What about you? Aren't you two sick of being such losers?

CAWWW!

CAWW!!

CAWW!!

AWWWKK!

We've got to get out of here. This way!

Are you sure you know how to drive?

Of course.

Whoaaa!

Watch out!

HONKKKK

You kids look awful. Hop in!

... and they keep them in a laboratory because they're contagious, only now everyone's sick! That's why we ran away... we've got to get help!

Okay, okay... shh, don't worry. Everything's going to be fine.

You mean, you believe us? We're not making it up...

Of course not. You know, I have a girl who's just about your age...

Camp
Fielding
Next Right

No! Wait—What
are you doing?!
You said you'd
take us—

VRRMM

SCREECH

Don't be too hard on them. You should just see my Juliet... she's a total drama queen!

It's the age, huh? Thanks!

Welcome back. You're just in time.

WELCOME TO PARENT'S DAY

I almost forgot what real food tasted like.

Well, it's for our parents, right?

We've got to tell them what's going on.

... only we can't.

Are you kidding? Why not?

Because... we'll sound crazy. That's why they're letting us see them... don't you get it?

...what should we do?

...Mom!

FWUMP

...Mom! Hey, Mom! Dad!

...I'm serious! I really, really miss you!

Oh yeah? How come I have trouble believing that?

C'mon... like when we watch soap operas together? Or when we go visit Aunt Carla? Or clothes shopping?

—it's true! I really, really want to become a doctor!

You said doctors were stupid...

That's why it's totally crucial I come home!

To become a candy striper?

Why don't we all get ready for the presentations?

Okay, Jenna?

$$2KI(aq) + Pb(NO_3)$$

MAZE

Aren't you going to take part in *anything?*

We don't believe in winners or losers at Camp Fielding. We believe in growth. And that's what we've been doing: growing!

Now here's a great guy, despite the fact that he's a *politician*—Senator Hal Braymin!

Thanks, my friend. Camp Fielding represents the future of education in our country. By improving test scores at privately funded camps like this, we reduce government spending—and cut taxes—while keeping achievement high for our kids.

I don't know. Michelle seemed so distant when I tried to kiss her...

Who cares? For the next Yo-Yo Ma, I'll take a little distant!

Look, Ma—you've got to listen to me...

No... you listen to me! I've had it up to here with your attitude! As far as I can tell, the whole time you been here, you haven't done a damn thing!

How do you think I feel, being the only one with a retard for a kid? You are gonna stay here and make something of yourself for once in your life! Otherwise, don't bother coming home. You got that?

Mom... please. Don't leave me here!!

Jenna. You're throwing away an incredible opportunity. Can't you see what this place is doing for everyone?

—But there's like this plague! And they're trying to keep it a secret... but it's spreading! We're all gonna die!

Well, at least it's not elves in your closet again!

Look. I think we've had enough fun and games from the two of you.

It's too late! We know all about the—

—oww!

No, let her finish. What do you know about?

—that everybody here has some kinda disease! And we're the only ones who don't have it... yet!

... What if I told you you were right?

What do you mean, it's really true?

... You've heard of Lyme Disease, right?

Sure... you get it from ticks.

There's a similar disease here... a very rare disease that, if not treated, is fatal.

Come on... I want to show you two something.

92

As you can understand, we'd just as soon not have this leak to the public. But we've been dealing with it very effectively... in-house.

So why were the counselors sneaking into our bunks at night?

They were giving innoculations. We've all had them, as well.

What about the ice cream?

A mild sedative and muscle relaxant. It's a large needle, and we didn't want to frighten anyone.

Then why is everyone acting like some kind of robot?

Okay... obviously, there have been some side-effects. But they're only temporary.

And what if we say no?

It's a free country. But then you'll run the very real risk of getting sick yourselves and maybe infecting your families. And of course, the disease... well, you might as well see for yourself.

...Is that Sherry and the others?

I'm afraid so. They didn't receive the innocula-tion.

We don't have any choice!

But how can we know for sure we'll really be okay?

We don't. But at least we'll be smart.

So ...

So maybe our parents will finally stop hating us so much.

The side effects are only temporary? Are you sure?

Two, three weeks. Tops.

Well... *gulp* does it hurt?

95

So how did Don finally get them to go along?

He told them it was a vaccine.

Really? What about the side effects?

He said they were temporary.

DO NOT ENTER

202

No... no!

There... hope that one takes.

You ready to do the girl?

Oh, man... not another one!

Let's just deal with it, okay?

We better call Don.

Now? But it's after three.

This one's bad. He's pretty far along.

TAP TAP TA

Owww.

TAPTAPTA

Jenna!

TAP TAP TA

See? And it's about to hatch.

Prematurely.

Great.

You hear something?

No.

Look—I don't care what anyone says. I can't lose another kid. Not after those three.

I'm gonna puke.

Quick... do some-thing. Give him CPR or something... and see if you can stop the bleeding.

But what about the... is it...

Dead.

I gotta get rid of it before you-know-who shows up. Keep your mouths shut.

105

What's happened?

First those three miscarriages. Then the two who escaped. So much has gone wrong, you make it hard to trust you.

Nothing! Everything's fine! I was just— peeing, that's all! You wouldn't understand!

You haven't been drinking again, have you?

No!

You know there'll be no payment if you are. Of course, I wouldn't be surprised. That's the reason you took the job in the first place, isn't it?

You don't have to be cruel.

Don't let us down. Every day, the pollution gets worse on my planet—our young are dying in record numbers. Our whole world depends on you.

I don't even *like* eggs, and now my head is one.

SNIFF

I can't believe we walked into their trap like a couple of big idiots...

C'mon... like who could have guessed what was really going on?

You mean that giant bird aliens are using our brains to hatch their young?

heh heh heh

hehe

sniff

And it's going to make us smarter, right?

Smarter zombies.

Do you feel anything yet?

No.

108

Awesome sunrise, huh guys?

It's no good... everyone's watching us.

I wish we knew how much time we have.

Hey, this is really good.

It's already started.

Come on. Let's get out of here.

Do you think it'll work?

It's worth a try. He usually takes half an hour for lunch.

Let's go.

"People," "Time," "Newsweek"...

Anything from around here?

Try "The Jamestown Gazette".

If we can just get one reporter into that lab... got it!

Okay... give me the phone number.

Cool... a geodesic dome.

Hey... let me try.

114

Lucas. They're winning... aren't they?

Says who?

Come on!

Hold on... this'll take a second.

Lucas...

BOYS'CABIN

GIRLS'CABIN

I'm just getting some stuff. Be right out...

How disorganized.

C'mon, c'mon, what's taking so long...?

I think they went this way!

Remember—no force! We want to bring them back safe and sound!

This area's covered. Let's head back to camp.

Revolting.

Lucas!

One second!

TAP TAP

What the—

"Calcium citrate bonded with titrate of magnesium." Holy crap...

Lucas... Lucas!

YANK

They're coming back!

It's no good. They're right behind us.

They didn't see us. We can still make it to the road.

So? What's gonna happen then? We can't outrun a car.

...You mean we can't outrun a car that's working.

I cut the line for the brake fluid and disconnected the alternator.

Now there's one thing you've gotta help me with...

Help me get this down.

It's going to be crude... but I think we can rig up a working model...

A working model of what?

Cabins 3, 4, and 5 are checking the perimeter.

Nothing on the cameras, and the bunks were empty.

Maybe it's better if they make it off campus, out in the open.

How do you figure?

They may be smart, but they're still kids. How far can they get on foot?

CAMP FIELDING

Wha—?

Quick... let's go.

... Who calibrated the steering?

There wasn't time! Without a gyroscope, I thought if we extrapolated the counterbalance, we could—

Hey, Jenna... JENNA...

AAAAAGHHHHHHH!

AAAGHHHHHHHHH!

Choke, rrrrrr, clunk.

Grind, gakk, phhhht.

It's an antidote some camper was working on before he went under... but it's incomplete.

We'll have to extrapolate based on what's there.

Can we compound the solution from common chemicals?

We have no choice.

BUY MORE

Stop... come back here!

We're going to need a secure location. With high-speed Internet access, phone lines...

Steady food supply, digital media equipment...

Back up, back up. You were *both* kicked out of the program?

Umm, not precisely...

But why didn't anyone call us?

Sorry. There's actually no time to explain...

Let's go.

Jenna? What are you doing?

What's going on?

I'm almost done with the calculations.

I'd say we have approximately two hours and forty-nine minutes left.

I still don't understand. With the others, personality transformation was almost instantaneous. Why is it taking us so long?

I was wondering that myself.

Uhh, Lucas... what's your mother's phone number?

Aren't you even going to tell us what happened?

Hey, pal... don't make me smack the answer out of you, I'm warning you...

It's a tri-nucleic acidic compound... why didn't I think of that?

Maybe we should call...?

That's what I was thinking. Come on...

We're narrowing it down. Let me try a different concentration...

CAMP FIELDING

Should we mix them now?

Too unstable. We should wait until we're ready.

All right... that's it. Party's over.

Believe us. It's for your own good...

You can yell and scream all you want...

We want you to take us back to Camp Fielding.

What?

There are other children we have to save.

And in a very short while, we won't care about anyone else.

I mean... well, that's great. We...

We thought you'd be mad or something...

I'm so proud of you, honey!

How you doing back there, honey?

Fine.

That's them.

Let's go.

SCREECH

127

Okay...as planned, we'll give 'em an escort.

So what did you and that guy talk about all night?

Oh, grown-up crap, that's all.

Oh, just contracts... pretty boring. You didn't miss much, honey.

She always knew.

They were in on it, the whole time.

Why does it feel like the process is accelerating so swiftly now?

Jenna.

Why don't I feel anything at all?

Lucas.

BRINGG

And make sure you take them into camp separately, too.

Are you sure that's necessary? She seems pretty far gone already.

We can't afford to take any more chances. That's what they told me.

Just do it, okay?

CRUNCH

Of course. Hormonal secretions triggered by feelings of affection and physical attraction were retarding the alterations of our brains...

...and slowing the diminishment of our individuality, defiance, etc. So Jenna and I had to be separated. How unfortunate.

And this has meant a cessation of our friendship. A shame.

... Jenna?

Hey!

Stay here. I'll be right back, okay?

Psssst...

Jenna... no! It's me!

Don't you understand? That's the reason we could fight it off so long... because we were *together*!

Let me go!

... Lucas?

Come on... there's no time!

Do you still have your half of the solution?

I believe so. But even after we combine them, how can we treat the greatest number of campers before being detected?

That's it. Total immersion... epidermal transmission.

T-days at two... and it's Thursday.

CLICK

... chem feeder, drains.

Basin, pump, filter...

So the water cycles from the pool through here—

—and back again. What am I, stupid?

Of course not.

SSSSSSHHH

What is it?

135

You've got to be kidding.

We don't have time to worry about them. It's late, as it is.

CAMP FIELDING

CAMP FIELDING
SUMMER OF LEARNING AND FUN

Let's get on with it.

I don't under-stand. Where are they going?

Oh, no...

Look at them.

We're too late.

What?

They're ready for hatching. They're going to the laboratory.

How do we stop them?

We can't. Except...

Except that baby birds instinctively follow the parental figure anywhere. Am I correct?

Absolutely.

?!

Whaaa- aaa...?

SPLASH

SPLASH

SPLASH.

KOFF KOFF

An animal's instinctive response to sudden sightlessness is immobilization... Am I correct?

Wha—??

Noooo!

Aiiiiieeeeee!

SPLASH

SSHHHH

KOFF KOFF
HRK
BLEAGH

Hey... what's going on?

Beats me.

CAMP FIELDING

Look— dead birdies.

Should we clean them up?

Gross.

Nah.

147

Jenna? Want some fresh-baked cookies?

No thanks, Mom!

TURN ON CNN JENNA

And now, I wanna introduce my choice for Secretary of Education...I call him "Egg head", but you all know him as former Senator Hal Braymin!

beep
beep